TELEVISION Teaches Too!

Dear Reader

The importance of learning about indigenous cultures is the main reason why I wrote this book. I am a descendant of New Zealand's Māori indigenous culture so my research started in my home country. I began by interviewing people at New Zealand's indigenous television station – Māori Television – about their programs for children and families. Their children's programs are creative, educational and a lot of fun!

TEAMS OF TALENTED PEOPLE PRODUCE INFORMATIVE AND ENTERTAINING PROGRAMS FOR MĀORI TELEVISION.

Then, the book takes you to Hawaii where two creative filmmakers have produced fascinating documentaries – one about the Hawaiian hula and the other about the best ukuleles in Hawaii!

Aloha!

Sharon Parsons

My sincere thanks to the following people for their time, information, images and enthusiasm for this book:

The team at Māori Television, Auckland, New Zealand

The team at Kura Productions, Auckland, New Zealand

The team at Tumanako Productions, Auckland, New Zealand

Lisette Flanary, Honolulu, Hawaii, USA

Dawn Kaniaupio, Honolulu, Hawaii, USA

The team at Kamaka Ukulele, Hawaii, USA

Contents

TELEVISION Teaches Too!

Part 1: World **Indigenous** Television

The term "indigenous peoples" refers to the first inhabitants of a region or country. In Australia, the Indigenous peoples are generally referred to as Aboriginal and Torres Strait Islander peoples. The Indigenous peoples of New Zealand are known as Māori. The Indigenous peoples of Canada are generally referred to as Aboriginal Canadians. In addition, cultural groups in a region or country may have different names.

Around the world, there are millions of people who are descendants of indigenous cultures. There are many ways in which their culture and language have been preserved for future generations.

Television is used to communicate indigenous language and culture. Some filmmakers and producers receive government funding to make television programs about indigenous history, traditions, culture and language.

ABORIGINAL

The word "aboriginal" is derived from the Latin term *ab origine*, meaning "from the beginning". It was first used in reference to the pre-Roman inhabitants of Latium, an ancient country in Italy.

playing the Aboriginal didgeridoo

1 World Indigenous Television Broadcasters Network (WITBN)

NEW ZEALAND

In 2008, the chief executive of New Zealand's Māori Television, Jim Mather, thought it would be a good idea for indigenous television stations around the world to get together. He invited representatives of indigenous television stations to New Zealand and they talked about how they could work together to retain and grow indigenous languages and cultures through television. They formed the World Indigenous Television Broadcasters Network (WITBN) and Jim Mather was appointed the first chairman. The WITBN includes members from places such as New Zealand, Australia, Taiwan, Scotland, Norway, Wales, Ireland, South Africa, Hawaii and Canada.

Jim Mather

An Indigenous Broadcasting World

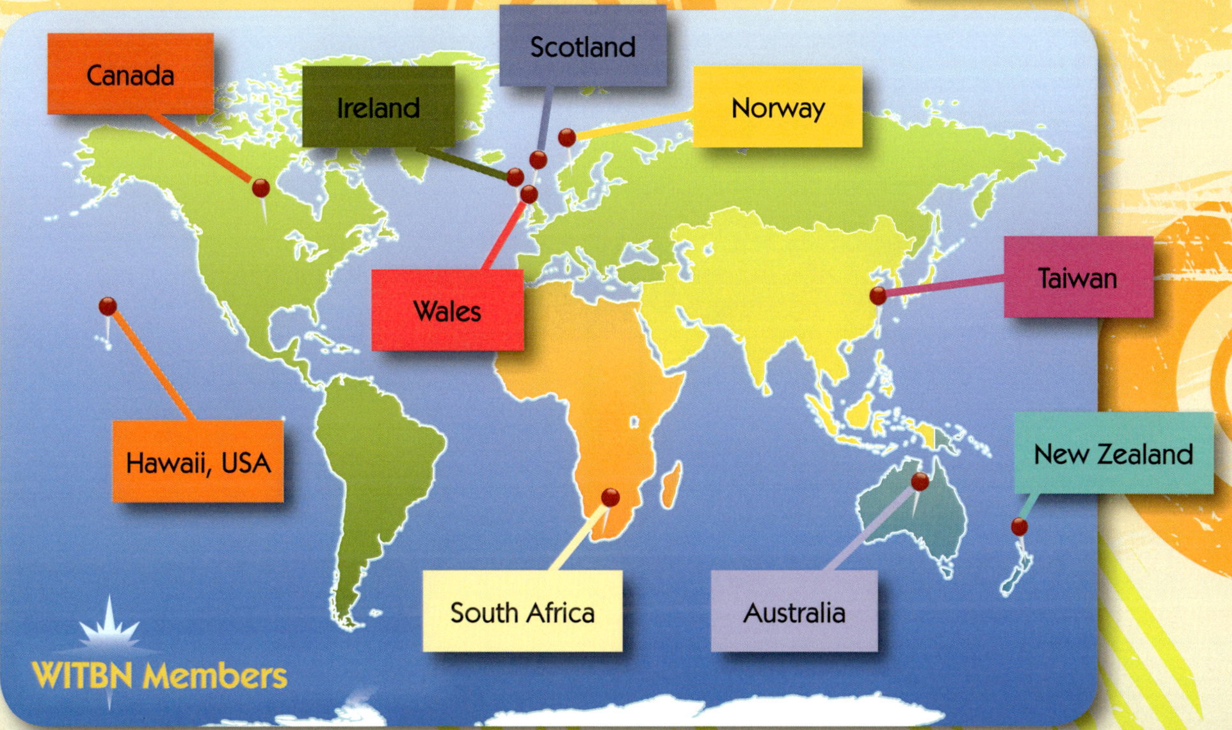

Part 2: Māori Television

Many people around the world may not know much about Māori culture in New Zealand, but they may have experienced the haka – an important expression of Māori culture. The New Zealand All Blacks rugby team always performs the *ka mate* haka before an international match. People who want to know more about Māori language and culture can check out Māori Television's website.

The All Blacks perform the ka mate *haka before each rugby match.*

Haka History

Traditionally, the haka was a show of strength before battle.

Traditionally, the haka was performed primarily by men. There were many occasions for haka: a welcome, an acknowledgement of achievements or as a show of strength before going into battle.

Māori warriors did the haka at battles.

While men performed the haka at battles, women protected their *pa* and their people by doing the haka to warn off enemies, too.

A modern haka welcomes guests.

Today, the haka is performed by New Zealanders at many official, cultural and sporting occasions.

Common Māori Greetings

If you are visiting New Zealand for the first time, here are some important Māori expressions that will show respect for the culture and language:

- *Hello* or *good luck*: **kia ora**
- *Hello* or *thanks* to one person: **tēnā koe**
- *Hello* or *thanks* to two people: **tēnā kōrua**
- *Hello* or *thanks* to three or more people: **tēnā koutou**
- *Goodbye*, said to someone leaving: **haere rā**
- *Goodbye*, said to someone staying: **e noho rā**

Find a Māori language website on the Internet and listen to the correct pronounciation of these words.

tēnā koe

tēnā koutou

kia-ora

tēnā kōrua

e noho rā

haere rā

a shell from a pāua, which is a shellfish found in New Zealand waters

2 Māori Television Starts Broadcasting

Māori Television began broadcasting programs in 2004 to enable all New Zealanders and visitors to learn more about Māori language and culture. The New Zealand Government funds Māori Television to produce high-quality programs.

MĀORI TELEVISION
mā rātou mā mātou mā koutou mā tātou

The Māori subtitle means "for them, for us, for you, for everyone".

Television Program Synopses

Television stations provide schedules so that people can check screening times for each program. Part of that process involves writing a short synopsis, or summary, for each program to entice viewers to watch. Sometimes writers don't have much space for each synopsis, so they have to be very skilled at capturing people's attention in one sentence.

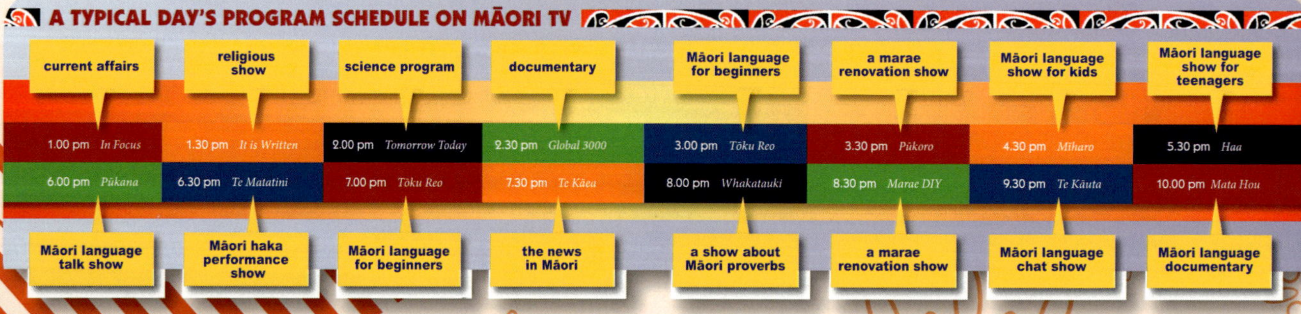

Interview with **Jim Mather**

As chief executive of Māori Television, Jim Mather manages about 170 people who create, produce and broadcast programs in Māori and English language every day.

"What is the key message that you want to get across with Māori Television?"

"As a broadcaster, I would like people to recognise that Māori language and culture is a unique part of our identity as New Zealanders. Māori Television has a role in sharing our language and culture with all New Zealanders in our country and around the world."

"How many hours of children's programs are broadcast on Māori Television?"

"Each week, Māori Television broadcasts about 16 hours of children's television programs. These programs are vitally important in helping children to learn and prosper as speakers of the Māori language. Our staff at Māori Television also conduct guided tours for groups, such as school groups and community sports groups."

"Do you broadcast non-Māori children's programs from overseas?"

"Yes, many of our children's shows are series of cartoons, so our editors translate the script into Māori. Then they replace the original soundtrack with a recording of the Māori script."

Pūkoro *presenters*

TAMARIKI

Tamariki in Māori language means "children".

3 Television Teaches *Te Reo* – Māori Language

Many people in New Zealand rely on Māori Television programs to improve their Māori language, or *te reo* Māori (te reo means "the language"). Thousands of New Zealanders living in other parts of the world can also follow the Māori language courses by logging onto the Māori Television website.

OUR MĀORI TELEVISION MOTTO IS '*MĀ TĀTOU*' WHICH MEANS 'FOR EVERYONE'.

JIM MATHER

The Pūkoro *presenters enjoy their job!*

Two *Te Reo* Programs

Kura Productions is a company that produces two popular series of *te reo* Māori programs for Māori Television: *Pūkoro* and *Tōku Reo*. *Pūkoro* is a fun and colourful *te reo* show for very young children. *Tōku Reo* means "My Language" in Māori, and the episodes allow the whole family to learn *te reo* every week.

Karen Waaka is the producer for both *Pūkoro* and *Tōku Reo*.

Tōku Reo *presenters (Raimona Peni (left) and Naomi Toilalo) make their television program presentation fun.*

the *Pūkoro* production team at work

Kura Productions

In 2004, Quinton Hita formed Kura Productions. Quinton has enjoyed a long career in television that has included acting, television and documentary production, and he is also an author of Māori language books. Quinton learnt Māori from his nannie (grandmother) from the age of 11.

Quinton Hita

AT MY NANNIE'S HOUSE, IF YOU DIDN'T SPEAK MĀORI, YOU DIDN'T GET FED! HAHA!

QUINTON HITA

Quinton on location, filming a new television program

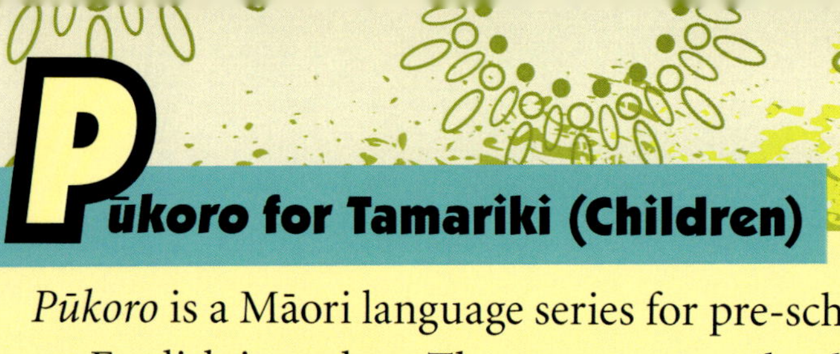

Pūkoro for Tamariki (Children)

Pūkoro is a Māori language series for pre-school children in New Zealand – no English is spoken. The presenters make the learning of Māori language fun by using colourful props, songs, stories and magic.

the Pūkoro *presenters before filming an episode*

Pūkoro = Pocket

Pūkoro means "pocket" in Māori. Clues for the show's language puzzles are found in the pockets of the *Pūkoro* Māori tiki characters.

Aniwa Nicholas

Ngatarawahi Fairhall

Presenters

Aniwa Nicholas

From left: Ngatarawahi Fairhall, Te Reweti, Tiare Tito, Aniwa Nicholas

From left: Aniwa Nicholas, Matutaera Ngaropo, Naomi Toilalo, Ngatarawahi Fairhall

Props

steady ... hold ...

action!

Production

rehearse ...

get ready ...

action!

4 *Tōku Reo* at 7.00

Every weeknight at 7.00 pm, thousands of New Zealand families watch *Tōku Reo* for half an hour. It has become a family tradition because everyone can learn new Māori words together with the help of two presenters, Raimona and Naomi. Another highlight of the program is the four funny actors who role-play the new words and grammar in comedy skits.

Language

The *Tōku Reo* Idea

Tōku Reo *is based on Professor John Moorfield's thoroughly researched Māori language course. He is a specialist in Māori language, literature and culture.*

Production Time Line

Each series of 50 episodes takes six months to create, write, produce and film. Many episodes are repeated so that people can continue to revise the Māori language.

A greenstone tiki (hei-tiki) is a carved human figure that is usually worn as a necklace.

Tōku Reo Team

On Camera

Naomi Toilalo and Raimona Peni present all the new words for each episode of Tōku Reo.

Four experienced actors reinforce the new Māori words in comedy role plays (Whakaari in Māori). From left: Wiremu Sarich, Kura Forrester, Hoete Mitai-Ngatai and Ross Mahuika Rawiri.

Off Camera

There are many people who work behind the scenes in production – here are some of them.

Mahu edits footage for each episode before it is ready to screen.

After many long hours working behind the scenes, production staff need time out, too. Rai and Heta enjoy a game of chess.

Raimona is a scriptwriter for Tōku Reo. *He writes the scripts for the role-plays, so it helps that he has a great sense of humour, too!*

Ten New Words from *Tōku Reo*

Every week, viewers of *Tōku Reo* learn ten new words as described below.

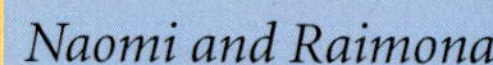

Naomi and Raimona

Monday Night

Raimona and Naomi present five new words in this order: Māori, English and again in Māori. It is helpful when people then hear elders use the words in Māori in the right context. The key is learning to listen and become familiar with the word.

Tuesday Night

Raimona and Naomi revise Monday's five new words. Viewers see each Māori word appear on the screen, hear it spoken in Māori and also see a role-play to reinforce learning.

Wednesday Night

Five new words are presented in the same format as Monday's program.

Thursday Night

Wednesday's five new words are revised. Then the program follows the same format as Tuesday. Viewers also get to see the second part of the role play.

Friday Night

The week's ten words are revised again in Māori, verbally and on screen. Viewers see a repeat of the role play.

Māori Greetings

kia ora	*e hoa*	*mā*	hello, friends
tēnā koutou	*e kare*	*mā*	hello, close friends
tēnā koutou	*e tamariki*	*mā*	hello, children
tēnā koutou	*e hine*	*mā*	hello, girls
tēnā koutou	*e tanē*	*mā*	hello, boys

Introducing New Māori Words

Māori Word	English Words	Repeat Māori Word
wini	win, victory	*wini*

Tōku Reo *role-play actors*

5 Marvellous *Mīharo*

Mīharo!

Mīharo is a magazine-style show that screens on Māori Television every weekday after school for children aged five to eight. The presenters are Huria Chapman and Whatanui Flavell. They do not speak English on the program because the show is designed to reinforce Māori language learnt at school.

Language

Mīharo Means?

In Māori, the word **mīharo** has many meanings. If **mīharo** is used as a verb, two of its meanings are "to wonder" or "to admire". If **mīharo** is used as an adjective, two of its meanings are "marvellous" and "amazing".

Whatanui Flavell and Huria Chapman

Meet the Producer of *Mīharo*

Kay Ellmers came up with the idea for *Mīharo* because there wasn't a television program to support students who were learning Māori language in schools. So, Kay created *Mīharo* and pitched her ideas to Māori Television. Today, this educational magazine-style show has become so successful it screens every day after school.

"I don't want children to sit passively and watch the show, so we involve kids at home, too," says Kay Ellmers.

Kay Ellmers (centre) with the presenters of Mīharo, *Huria Chapman and Whatanui Flavell.*

The Presenters of *Mīharo*

The presenters of *Mīharo* have energetic personalities and they present the show in a fun way. Huria Chapman was a secondary school teacher and Whatanui Flavell joined the show after secondary school at the age of 18.

Huria and Whatanui relax with an old friend in between filming segments.

Huria and Whatanui have fun in between filming segments.

In the Studio

clapper board

Whatanui rehearses in front of the green screen

A GREEN SCREEN

A green screen (or blue screen) is a screen that provides a backdrop for filming a presenter or actor. This technique allows the editor or director to add other images around the presenter on the green areas, such as props, a map or characters.

The director works with Huria and Whatanui.

The director works with Huria and Kay.

Mīharo in Schools

Many of the *Mīharo* segments are filmed in schools where Māori language is spoken and taught in class. The students get a chance to present some of the segments in Māori.

Students listen to the producer's instructions.

Students are interviewed and filmed.

Students present a report for the program.

New Māori Words from *Mīharo*

Sometimes, the *Mīharo* writers have to create new Māori words for new products, sports and technology.

gelato

From "Ice-Cream" to "Gelato" to "Sorbet"

Aihikirimi is the Māori word for "ice-cream".

Since gelato is more dense or thicker than most ice-creams, the *Miharo* writers created the term *aihikirimi kuku* for "gelato". *Kuku* is the Māori word for "dense" or "thick".

a Māori canoe (waka)

The Māori term created for sorbet was *aihikirimi huarākau* because sorbet is mainly made up of fruit puree. *Huarākau* is Māori for "fruit".

From Canoe to Land Yacht

In Māori language, the word for "canoe" is *waka*. Creating the Māori term for "land yacht" (*waka panahau*) involved three stages: *waka* (canoe or vehicle) + *pana* (pushed by) + *hau* (wind).

a land yacht at speed

Animating Myths and Legends

Mīharo animators create a 90-second animation for each episode about Māori myths and legends.

Rehua is a sacred personage who lives in the highest heaven, and some Māori legends refer to him as a star.

Mukukai is a *taniwha*, or a water creature, in Māori folklore.

a still from an animated scene depicting the connection between our spiritual realm and our physical realm – the spiritual realm is represented by the pink-toned animation above.

A MĀORI SPIRITUAL BELIEF

In this scene, animators visually told the story of a Māori spiritual belief that a soul or spirit enters the physical realm by way of the human form (baby) at conception.

Rata and His Canoe

"Rata and His Canoe" is one of the most popular Māori legends. It was animated for an episode of *Mīharo*. An abridged version is retold below.

"Rata" is the name of a Māori native tree. In the Māori legend, a man named Rata was perplexed because the tree he cut down had mysteriously regrown.

One day, the family of Rata told him to build a large canoe so he could travel across the seas to collect his father's bones from a distant place. As a mark of respect, his family wanted Rata to arrange a burial of his father's bones at the village. Rata searched a nearby forest for a very large tree. Before too long, he discovered the perfect tree and used his imagination to "see" the canoe in the tree trunk.

The next day, Rata returned to the forest and cut down the tree. As night fell, Rata went home and decided to carve his canoe the following day.

The forests belonged to Tāne, the Maori god of the forests. The children of Tāne, in the form of birds, insects and spirits, immediately descended on every part of the fragmented tree. Together, they reassembled the tree and replanted it.

The next morning, Rata returned to the exact spot where he had left the felled tree. He couldn't believe what he saw before him. But he didn't have time to wonder what had happened, so he felled the tree again. That evening, Rata left the forest with a heavy feeling of tiredness. But, as soon as he was out of sight, the same group of birds, insects and spirits reassembled and replanted the tree.

Imagine how Rata felt the following morning on returning to the forest! However, he was a patient man and he decided to fell the tree – one last time. When night closed in on the forest, Rata pretended to leave. Instead, he crept back and crouched down in a hiding place.

When Rata saw the children of Tāne start assembling the tree the forest, he rushed out from behind the bushes and shouted, "What are you doing to my tree?"

The children of the forest replied, "The tree belongs to Tāne and you didn't ask for his permission to cut it down."

TĀNE

Tāne is the Māori god of the forests. The birds, insects and spirits that lived in the forests were called the children of Tāne or the children of the forest.

Rata felt so ashamed that he hung his head and couldn't speak. The birds, insects and spirits felt sorry for him, and ordered him to return to the forest at first light.

When Rata arrived at the forest, he saw the most magnificently carved canoe. The children of the forest were nowhere to be seen but, as a sign of gratitude, Rata left some gifts for them.

a Māori canoe (called a waka*)*

Finally, Rata was able to heave the canoe down to the sea for his important voyage.

7 Should the Silver Ferns Be Allowed to Perform the Men's *Ka Mate* Haka?

TEXT TYPE
Discussion

The haka is a ceremonial Māori dance form traditionally performed mostly by men. The most well-known is the *ka mate* haka, made famous by New Zealand premier rugby team, the All Blacks. They have performed the *ka mate* haka before each match for over one hundred years. Other men's sports teams, such as New Zealand's men's basketball team (the Tall Blacks), have also performed the haka at international matches.

In 2011, members of New Zealand's national women's netball team, the Silver Ferns, indicated their intention to start performing the *ka mate* haka at the World Netball Championships later in the year. Public opinion on this issue has been divided.

The All Blacks rugby team perform the ka mate *haka before a match.*

Some people believe that as the *ka mate* haka is widely recognised as a New Zealand cultural icon, its performance should not be limited to men. All New Zealanders have the right to express pride in their heritage, regardless of their gender or background. As New Zealand's most successful women's sports team, the Silver Ferns feel that they are entitled to perform the *ka mate* haka before their games. For them, it is an expression of their pride in representing New Zealand on the world stage.

Supporters of this view think that allowing the Silver Ferns to perform the *ka mate* haka would help to build team spirit. Having good team morale is very important for success. Furthermore, if the Silver Ferns performed the *ka mate* haka at the World Netball Championships, it would increase publicity for netball around the world.

New Zealand's Silver Ferns netball team compete against Australia's national netball team, known as the Diamonds.

Will the Silver Ferns join the All Blacks by starting games with a haka?

The Silver Ferns' performance of the *ka mate* haka would also show that men and women are equally capable. For some people this last point is vital, given the importance of positive role models, both female and male, for young people.

However, not everyone agrees that the Silver Ferns should perform the *ka mate* haka. One reason for this is that it has traditionally been performed by men, so allowing women to perform it may be regarded as disrespectful of Māori culture.

In addition, the Silver Ferns can express pride in their national identity by performing a women's haka. Worldwide audiences would certainly enjoy this and it would increase people's understanding that the *ka mate* haka is just one example of the haka dance form.

By performing another haka, there would be an increased global understanding that Māori culture is multi-dimensional.

There are differing opinions about whether the Silver Ferns should perform the *ka mate* haka at the World Netball Championships. Some people believe that the *ka mate* haka should continue to be performed by men only. Others believe that women should be able to perform it, too. These views seem to focus on ideas about national identity and cultural traditions. But the important thing to consider is not who is performing the *ka mate* haka, but that every performance is done with respect and in the spirit of the Māori culture that it represents.

Part 3: Indigenous **Television** in Hawaii

Hawaii has a long and rich history of tradition and culture. When people think about Hawaii, some of the first images that come to mind are the Hawaiian hula and the ukulele.

Hula is the ancient art of storytelling through Hawaiian dance. The ukulele is a Hawaiian instrument developed in the late 1800s. In recent years, two Hawaiian filmmakers have produced successful documentaries about the hula and the ukulele.

a modern hula dancer and a ukulele musician

Pacific Islanders in Communications

Pacific Islanders in Communications is an indigenous television network for audiences in Hawaii, USA. The organisation provides filmmakers with an opportunity to screen their documentaries and films about Hawaiian culture and language.

traditional hula

Communication

Oiwi TV

Oiwi TV is the only native Hawaiian television station that offers Hawaiian audiences a wide selection of programs, including news, documentaries, cartoons and language lessons.

8 A Hawaiian Hula Documentary

Lisette Marie Flanary was born in the USA but she spent the summers with family in Honolulu, Hawaii. Today, Lisette is a successful documentary filmmaker who lives in New York, in the USA. In 2005, Lisette decided to make a film about men who enjoy doing the hula. Why? She says, "Most people think that only women do the Hawaiian hula, so I wanted to dispel those misconceptions."

Lisette on location in Hawaii

Lisette filming Na Kamalei *in Hawaii*

Na Kamalei *perform at the world's biggest hula competition in Hawaii.*

HAWAIIAN MEANINGS

Halau is Hawaiian for "school".

Na kamalei is Hawaiian for "the lei of children".

"MEN DO HULA, TOO!
LISETTE FLANARY"

Hula Documentary

Lisette decided that her new documentary would feature a master hula teacher, Robert Cazimero, and his *halau* of male hula dancers. The documentary follows Robert and the hula dancers as they practise their performance for the world's biggest hula competition.

Robert Cazimero (centre) with Lisette (right) and a crew member

Lisette gets ready to film Na Kamalei.

Robert Cazimero and his Na Kamalei

First prize in the men's hula category is a highly desired honour at the hula competition. The documentary ends on a happy note because Robert Cazimero's *Halau Na Kamalei* won the *Kane* (Hawaiian for "men") hula competition.

Lisette concentrates on filming Na Kamalei.

Oli and Hula

Ancient Hawaiian history was not written down. Instead, history in the form of stories was passed from generation to generation orally, often through a traditional chanting called *oli*.

Ancient hula is called *kahiko* and the hula dancers perform to the chanting sounds of *oli* and the traditional sounds of drumming. The hula dancer's hand and body movements describe words and aspects of nature from the *oli* chants.

an ancient hula from 1827

Modern Hula

A modern style of hula is called *auana*, which is based on the movements of the ancient hula. The dancers use more fluid, graceful movements and wear more elaborate costumes and leis.

The dance is performed to the sounds of modern musical instruments that include the ukulele, guitar and bass guitar.

Hula dancers have always worn leis, bracelets and necklaces.

HULA GODDESS

Laka is Hawaii's goddess of hula.

9 A Hawaiian Ukulele Documentary

Dawn Kaniaupio lives in Hawaii and she is a successful producer of documentaries about Hawaiian culture and language. Dawn is passionate about her Hawaiian culture so she decided to make a film about the history and tradition of ukulele craftsmanship in one famous family.

Dawn Kaniaupio

a Portuguese cavaquinho *guitar*

The First Ukuleles

Portuguese migrants first brought their own instruments, which looked like ukuleles, to Hawaii in 1879. Manuel Nunes was one of the Portuguese migrants who came to work in Hawaii's sugar cane fields. At the time, Manuel and two other Portuguese instrument makers invented and made the Hawaiian ukulele by using some of their design ideas from Portugal.

Hawaiians enjoyed listening to the ukulele's unique sounds and it soon became Hawaii's most popular musical instrument. Everyone learnt the art of playing the ukulele.

A great demand for ukuleles followed and Manuel Nunes could not keep up with it. He took on an apprentice named Samuel Kamaka, who later formed his own company, Kamaka Ukulele and Guitar Works.

Samuel Kamaka

Heart Strings: The Story of the Kamaka Ukulele

The Kamaka family is world-famous for making the best ukuleles in Hawaii. The original skill and artistry of making a ukulele by hand has been passed from generation to generation for over 100 years. Every serious musician who plays the ukulele wants an original Kamaka ukulele, but they have to wait for many months because the family still crafts them by hand.

Casey Kamaka (a luthier) and his nephew Dustin Kamaka (right) make and fix ukuleles. together.

Kamaka Ukeleles Use Koa

The Kamaka family craft each ukulele out of a local wood called "koa".

the koa tree

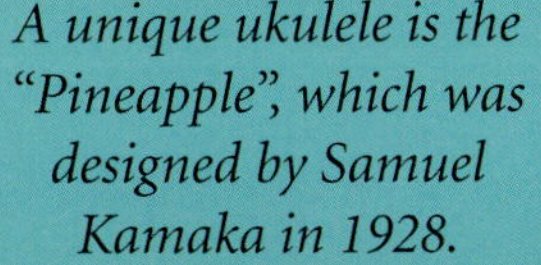

A unique ukulele is the "Pineapple", which was designed by Samuel Kamaka in 1928.

Sam Kamaka Jr and Herbert Ohta designed the Concert Bell-Shaped Deluxe ukulele in 1965.

Index

Glossary

documentary A movie about something that is real

legends Popular stories about things that may have happened a long time ago.

leis Necklaces that are made of flowers

marae A Māori word meaning a place that is very important to Māori people

Pacific Islanders The original inhabitants of a group of islands in the Pacific Ocean, including Hawaii and New Zealand

personage A formal way of describing an important person or a legendary figure

synopsis A short summary of what happens in a television program

tiki A wooden or stone carving of a person

tradition Something that has been done for a very long time